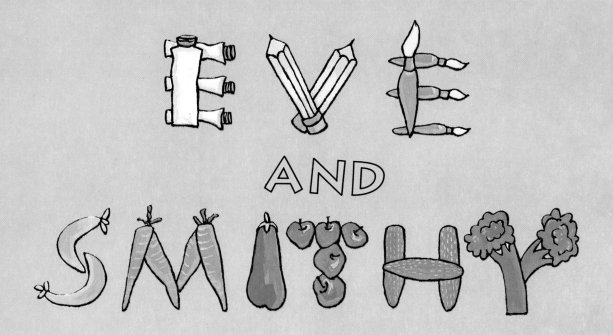

EVE AND SMITHY

To Hans and Astrid

good friends and good neighbors

And with butterflies for Flory

Library of Congress Cataloging in Publication
Edwards, Michelle: Eve and Smithy : an Iowa tale / by Michelle Edwards. p.   cm.
Summary: Smithy tries to think of a gift for Eve, his neighbor who gardens and
paints pictures of Iowa. ISBN 0-688-11825-9. — ISBN 0-688-11826-7 (lib. bdg.)
{1. Friendship—Fiction. 2. Gardening—Fiction. 3. Artists—Fiction. 4. Iowa—Fiction.}
I. Title. PZ7.E262Ev 1995 {E}—dc20 92-44166 CIP AC

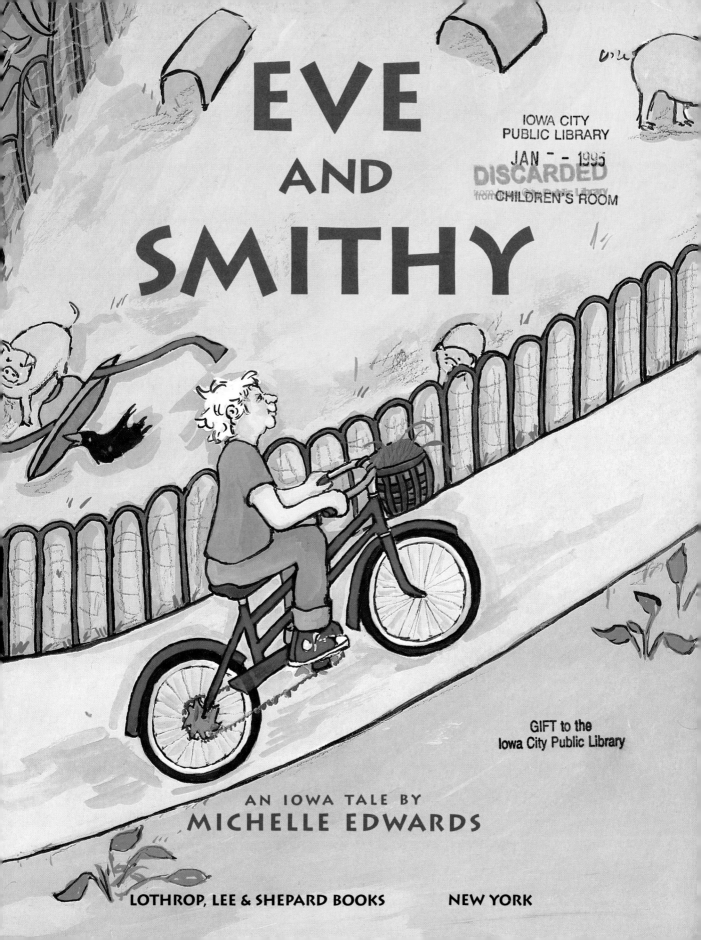

EVE
AND
SMITHY

AN IOWA TALE BY
MICHELLE EDWARDS

LOTHROP, LEE & SHEPARD BOOKS   NEW YORK

On the corner of Dodge and Dubuque, past four corn-fields, seventeen pigs, and a university, is Eve's house. It's old and purple, and in the back is an enormous garden full of dandelions and vegetables. Eve says that all those vegetables keep her young, and that there is nothing in this whole wide world better than a cup of dandelion tea.

When Eve isn't in her garden weeding and mulching, she is in her studio, painting. Sometimes she gets so busy painting that she almost forgets about her garden.

But Smithy, her neighbor, never forgets. Every day he checks on Eve's vegetables.

"Mulch around those peppers," he tells her. "Weed those carrots and pick those peas." And Smithy is always right.

Every fall Eve goes to her studio to paint something for Smithy, a thank-you-for-a-good-harvest painting.

When she is finished, she calls on Smithy. "Best hang this one on the living room wall near the door," she announces. And Eve is always right about where her paintings should be hung.

Before Smithy met Eve, he never owned any art. Now he has a whole houseful, all from Eve, of course. Every night after dinner, he looks at Eve's paintings. The blue one in the corner of his living room always reminds him of the blue sky hanging over his cornfields back when he used to farm. And he is sure that the mostly red painting is about his prize-winning tomatoes. When he turns that painting upside down, he can almost see the blue ribbon.

"Thanks to Eve, I've got windows on the whole, wide world," declared Smithy one night. "I think the time has come for me to give *her* something. Something special."

Smithy had shared his best recipes with Eve, told her when to harvest her vegetables, and let her pick all the dandelions she wanted from his yard, but he had never given her a *real* present. As he turned on the farm report, he began to think about what that present might be. A radio, maybe? No, Eve said that radios didn't let you hear the birds sing, the cicadas chirp, or the wind howl.

Smithy thought all evening long. The next morning he made himself a big pot of coffee, filled his thermos, and went outside to think some more. A coffee pot? No, Eve didn't drink coffee, only that yellowy dandelion tea of hers. A teapot then? No, according to Eve, tea should be brewed one cup at a time.

Old Eve was a tough one all right. Smithy thought
about her present while he drank his coffee, and turned
the compost heap, and checked on his bread dough. He
thought while he climbed the ladder to prune his apple
tree. Then he looked down to check on Eve's garden.
And there was Eve, without a hat, in the noonday sun.
Smithy could see her face turning red from the heat.

"When will Eve learn about the Iowa sun? How many
times have I told her to wear a hat?" said Smithy. Then
he stopped short.

He knew the perfect gift for Eve. He wrapped it in the Sunday paper and walked next door.

"Good afternoon, Eve," he called.
Eve looked up from her cabbage patch.
"I've been thinking a lot about all that you have given
me with your art and your friendship. I wanted to give
you something too, and that's not an easy thing to do."
He handed her the package.

"It's my lucky DeKalb," said Smithy as Eve opened her gift. "Every year that I wore this cap to the State Fair, my tomatoes won first prize. I wore this cap the night Bessie gave birth to our twins. It's a lucky cap, Eve, and I want you to have it. It's perfect for the Iowa sun, and it might work wonders for your garden too."

"I've always admired this cap," said Eve as she tried it on. Then she gave Smithy a big hug. "A perfect fit. I promise to wear it in the sun. Maybe in the rain too."

Smithy grinned.

That evening while she painted in her studio, Eve was certain she could hear the rabbits in her garden packing for Kansas, her tomatoes fattening right on the vine, and her tiny cucumbers perking right up.

"Not to mention the fact," she told Smithy the next day, "that there's nothing like a friend's lucky seed cap for swatting flies."

Michelle Edwards was born in Bridgeport, Connecticut, and grew up in upstate New York. She earned her B.A. at S.U.N.Y. Albany, and studied art at the Bazalel Art Academy in Jerusalem and at the University of Iowa in Iowa City. She lingered in Iowa for eight years, and it was there that she met and married her husband, Rody. "Iowa is a lovely place," she says, "where it's possible to meet all kinds of people—poets and artists and farmers and puppeteers, to name just a few. It's a place where being a good neighbor is still important." Eve and Smithy in this book are a composite of some of the people she knew and loved in Iowa.

Michelle now lives in St. Paul, Minnesota, where her time is taken up by her children and her career as a writer and illustrator. Her books include *Chicken Man*, which won the 1992 Jewish Book Award, *A Baker's Portrait, Alef-Bet: A Hebrew Alphabet Book*, and *Blessed Are You: Traditional Everyday Hebrew Prayers*. Her greatest fans and toughest critics are her three young daughters, Meera, Flory, and Lelia.